BRIGHT and EARLY BOOKS for BEGINNING Beginners

A Bright & Early Book

THE BERENSTAIN BEARS AND THE
SPOOKY OLD TREE

Stan and Jan Berenstain

from BEGINNER BOOKS   A Division of Random House, Inc.

Copyright © 1978
by Stanley and Janice Berenstain.

All rights reserved under
International and Pan-American
Copyright Conventions.
Published in the United States
by Random House, Inc., New York,
and simultaneously
in Canada by Random House
of Canada Limited, Toronto.

Library of Congress Cataloging in Publication Data:

Berenstain, Stanley
The Berenstain bears and the spooky old tree.

(A Bright and early book; BE23)
SUMMARY: One by one, three brave little bears
have second thoughts about exploring the interior of
a spooky old tree.
[1. Bears—Fiction] I. Berenstain, Janice,
joint author.   II. Title.
PZ7.B4483Bek   [E]   77-93771
ISBN 0-394-83910-2
ISBN 0-394-93910-7 lib. bdg.

Manufactured in the United States of America

Three little bears.

One with a light.
One with a stick.
One with a rope.

A spooky old tree.

Do they dare go into
that spooky old tree?

Yes.
They dare.

Three little bears...
One with a light.
One with a stick.
One with a rope.

A twisty old stair.

Do they dare go up
that twisty old stair?

Yes.
They dare.

Three little bears.
One with a light.
One with a stick.
And <u>one</u> with the shivers.

A giant key.

A moving wall.

Will the three little bears
go through that wall?
Do they dare go into
that spooky old hall?

Yes.
They dare.

Three little bears.
One with a light.
And <u>two</u> with the shivers.

Great Sleeping Bear.

Do they dare go over
Great Sleeping Bear?

Do they dare?
Well...

They came into the tree.

They climbed the stair.

They went through the wall...

and into the hall.

So of course they went over
Great Sleeping Bear!

Three little bears…
without a light,
without a stick,
without a rope.
And <u>all</u> with the shivers!

How will they ever
get out of there?

Three little bears
running fast.

Home again.
Safe at last.

Stan and Jan Berenstain

For years Stan and Jan Berenstain were well known to millions of adult readers for their many marvelously funny books and magazine features on family life in America. Then, with THE BIG HONEY HUNT, children discovered that they also wrote marvelously funny books about family life in Bear Country. Since then millions of beginning readers have enjoyed the misadventures of the famous Bear Family.

The Berenstains went to the same art school (the Philadelphia Museum School), enjoy the same food, tastes and hobbies, have the same two sons, and as far as can be discovered, type simultaneously on the same typewriter and draw simultaneously on the same piece of paper. They work together in the same studio in Bucks County, Pennsylvania, creating words and pictures that delight bears and children around the world.